W9-DGB-468

HOT

Celebrity Biographies

Justin Timberlake

BREAKOUT MUSIC SUPERSTAR

TONY NAPOLI

 Enslow Publishers, Inc.
40 Industrial Road
Box 398

Library of Congress Cataloging-in-Publication Data
Napoli, Tony.
  Justin Timberlake : breakout music superstar / by Tony Napoli.
      p. cm. — (Hot celebrity biographies)
  Includes bibliographical references and index.
  Summary: "Read about Justin Timberlake's life—from his early tv days to 'N Sync and a solo career"--Provided by
publisher.
  ISBN-13: 978-0-7660-3566-9
  ISBN-10: 0-7660-3566-2
  1. Timberlake, Justin, 1981-—Juvenile literature. 2. Rock musicians—United States—Biography—Juvenile literature. I.
Title.
  ML3930.T58N37 2009
  782.42164092--dc22
  [B]
                            2008051094

Paperback ISBN-13: 978-0-7660-3632-1
Paperback ISBN-10: 0-7660-3632-4

Printed in the United States of America

10 9 8 7 6 5 4 3 2 1

To our readers: We have done our best to make sure all Internet Addresses in this book were active and appropriate when we went to press. However, the author and the publisher have no control over and assume no liability for the material available on those Internet sites or on other Web sites they may link to. Any comments or suggestions can be sent by e-mail to comments@enslow.com or to the address on the back cover.

♻ Enslow Publishers, Inc., is committed to printing our books on recycled paper. The paper in every book contains 10% to 30% post-consumer waste (PCW). The cover board on the outside of each book contains 100% PCW. Our goal is to do our part to help young people and the environment too!

Photographs: Dan Steinberg/AP Images, 1; Lucy Nicholson/AP Images, 4; Matt Sayles/AP Images, 7, 11; Kevork Djansezian/AP Images, 9; Stephen Chernin/AP Images, 12; Fred Duval/FilmMagic/Getty Images, 15; Jeff Kravitz/FilmMagic/Getty Images, 17; Mark J. Terrill/AP Images, 20, 23, 28; Chris O'Meara/AP Images, 24; Kim D. Johnson/AP Images/Getty Images, 27; Peter Morrison/AP Images, 31; Richard Lewis/AP Images, 33; Evan Agostini/AP Images, 34; Todd Yates/AP Images, 37; Denis Poroy/AP Images, 39; John McConnico/AP Images, 43

Cover photo: Justin Timberlake attends a movie premiere in 2008.
Dan Steinberg/AP Images.

Contents

Young and Talented

Justin Timberlake stepped out on stage. He had his twelve-piece band with him. He was in Amsterdam, Holland. The crowd was excited. He was getting ready to play some songs from his new solo album. This was in September 2006.

Timberlake was a long way from home, the small town of Millington, Tennessee. He was also a long way from the child star of *The Mickey Mouse Club* that he had been. And he was even a long way from being a teenage pop star. The music he played that night was nothing like the music he made when he was a member of the boy band 'N Sync.

Sitting in the balcony in Amsterdam was his mother, Lynn. She had been coming to his shows for a long time. That night, she told a magazine writer she could even remember when she first noticed that her son could sing.

◄ *Justin Timberlake presenting an award at the Teen Choice Awards when he was a member of 'N Sync*

"We were coming home from a bluegrass festival in Mississippi with my brother and sister-in-law," she recalled. "All of a sudden my brother said, 'Is anyone listening to him?' . . . Justin was adding a harmony to the songs on the radio. He was [only] two!"

When the show ended, the crowd screamed and applauded. Of course, Lynn had seen this reaction before. She saw it back when Justin first stepped on stage in elementary school.

AN EARLY START

The first time Justin performed in front of an audience, he was in the third grade. He and some friends put on a talent show. The plan was to dance and lip-synch to some songs.

As the songs played, however, Justin did more than just move his lips. He began to sing too. Lynn had brought a camera to videotape the show. Afterward, she decided to talk to local singing teacher Bob Westbrook.

Justin's mother showed Westbrook the tape. He agreed to take Justin on as a student. Lynn wasn't surprised. Justin had been around music from the day he was born.

▲ *Justin Timberlake attends the premiere of the movie* The Love Guru *on June 11, 2008.*

A MUSICAL FAMILY

Justin was born on January 31, 1981. His parents, Randall Timberlake and Lynn Bomar, married very young. Lynn was twenty when Justin was born. The marriage didn't last long. Lynn and Randall divorced when Justin was three.

JUSTIN AT A GLANCE

Full name: Justin Randall Timberlake

Birthday: January 31, 1981

Nickname: JT

Height: 6 feet 2 inches

Favorite color: Blue

Favorite food: Breakfast cereal

Enjoys: Golfing, skiing, and snowboarding

Collects: Sports jerseys and sneakers

Fears: Snakes, sharks, and spiders

Still, Justin grew up in a close-knit family.

Musical talent seemed to be in Justin's genes. Justin's grandfather, Bill Bomar, was a guitarist. When Justin was two years old, he had a toy guitar he liked to carry everywhere. Justin's father, Randall, played guitar too. Randall also had a good singing voice, and he was the leader of his church choir.

Justin also happened to be raised in an area rich in musical history. He grew up in Millington, Tennessee. It is about twenty miles north of Memphis. The city is filled with many music clubs. Rhythm and blues legends such as Ike Turner, Howlin' Wolf, and B. B. King all got their starts there.

When Justin was five, his mother married Paul Harless, a banker. They lived in a middle-class home in Shelby Forest, a neighborhood in Millington. Justin became quite close to his new stepfather.

Overall, Justin had a happy childhood. In elementary school, he was an excellent student. Like many other kids his age, he loved video games and sports, especially basketball.

WINNING CONTESTS

Bob Westbrook, Justin's singing teacher, soon realized his new student had strong potential. All Justin needed was some formal training.

▶ *Justin Timberlake performs at the ESPY Awards in 2008.*

9

Westbrook urged Justin to sing at church, school, and even the mall. By the time Justin was ten, he had become fairly well known in the community. Soon, Justin began entering—and winning—junior talent contests throughout Tennessee. In August 1992, he entered a contest in Nashville. It was called the Universal Charm Pageant. Justin competed as a singer.

Justin sang the classic soul ballad, "When a Man Loves a Woman." He knocked the judges out. He took home first prize. It was $16,000 worth of savings bonds.

Justin's mother thought the time was right to try advancing her son's career. She learned that *Star Search* was holding auditions at a mall in Memphis. *Star Search* was a national TV talent show. Justin competed against about 500 others to win a chance to appear on the show. And he made it! Justin and his mother went to Orlando, Florida, where the show was filmed.

Justin spent a lot of time rehearsing for *Star Search*. In the first round, he was awarded three and a quarter stars, but his competitor received four. Naturally, he and his mother were very disappointed by the loss.

Justin didn't know it at the time, but losing *Star Search* turned out to be a lucky break for him. While in Orlando, Lynn heard about another TV show filmed there that was holding auditions. Tryouts were being held near Nashville,

▲ *Justin Timberlake is pictured at the MTV Movie Awards in 2006.*

Tennessee. Justin and Lynn flew there for the first tryout. If Justin were chosen, he would become a member of a very select club of young TV stars. He was going to audition for a role as a "Mouseketeer" on Disney's *The All New Mickey Mouse Club*.

Mouseketeer to Pop Star

Timberlake easily made it past the first tryout to become a Mouseketeer. A few weeks later, he took part in a second audition. He had to perform a routine with singing, dancing,

▲ When 'N Sync was forming, Chris Kirkpatrick (left) suggested bringing Justin Timberlake on board.

and making a speech. Timberlake scored quite well. He made the cut for the show's next season.

The All New Mickey Mouse Club, or *MMC*, was starting its sixth season in 1993. It was very popular with young people. The show featured various child actors. They would sing, dance, and perform in comedy sketches. It was filmed in Orlando, Florida, from April until September. Then the shows began airing on television in October.

This schedule meant Justin and his mother would have to live in Orlando during those months. So, they packed up and headed for Orlando. Justin was barely twelve years old.

TWO EDUCATIONS AT ONCE

The show's cast members were between eleven and eighteen years old. All the school-age members had to continue their education while they worked. Tutors taught them for at least three hours per day, five days per week. The courses had to be approved by the student's hometown school.

The Mouseketeers took dance classes and singing lessons. They practiced acting. The hours were long, and the work

THE MICKEY MOUSE CLUB

Walt Disney Productions created the original *The Mickey Mouse Club* show in 1955. It aired until 1959. *The Mickey Mouse Club* was a variety show, meaning it featured a variety of different segments. These included cartoons, music, talent, and comedy portions. The show's performers were teenagers called Mouseketeers.

The show was revived in the 1970s, and featured disco theme music and more minority cast members. However, it was not as popular as the original and did not air for long.

Despite this, The Disney Channel created a new version of the show that ran from 1989 to 1994. It was called *The All New Mickey Mouse Club*, but people often referred to it as just *MMC*. Several of today's popular stars got their starts on *MMC*. One of these, of course, was Justin Timberlake. Other Mouseketeers included singers Britney Spears and Christina Aguilera, actor Ryan Gosling, actress Keri Russell, and 'N Sync member JC Chasez. Singer Jessica Simpson also tried out but didn't make the cast.

was hard. But it was worth it. By the end of October 1993, *The Mickey Mouse Club* had filmed thirty-five shows.

That fall, Timberlake returned home. He also went back to E. E. Jeter Elementary School. Despite his new fame as a TV star, Timberlake hadn't changed much. He remained friendly and well liked.

During the fall and winter, Justin performed in many local events. He sang at both school and community shows. It was clear that he had gotten even better as a result of his time on *MMC*.

A SECOND AND FINAL SEASON

The following April, Timberlake and his mother returned to Orlando for the next season of *MMC*. When the season ended, Timberlake returned home again. Everyone in the cast thought the show would be back for another season. Its ratings were still pretty good. However, in February, Disney announced the show would not return for another season.

Like everyone else, Timberlake was disappointed. He had enjoyed his time on *MMC*. He had learned a lot about show business. And he had become good friends with at least one of his fellow Mouseketeers— Britney Spears.

PLANNING THE NEXT MOVE

Timberlake finished the 1995 school year at E. E. Jeter Elementary. One day Timberlake

▶ *Justin Timberlake is pictured at an 'N Sync concert in London in 1997.*

15

got a telephone call from Chris Kirkpatrick. Kirkpatrick was a singer. Kirkpatrick had been working with Lou Pearlman, a man who put together new music groups.

Pearlman already had helped create one act. It was a boy band called the Backstreet Boys. At this time, the Backstreet Boys weren't very well known. But within a short time, they would become one of the biggest pop groups in the world.

Pearlman wanted to form another five-person group. He asked Kirkpatrick to suggest some other candidates for the band. Living in Orlando, Kirkpatrick knew all about *MMC*. And he had been impressed with Timberlake's talent. So he asked Timberlake if he wanted to audition for the new group. Timberlake jumped at the chance. He, his mother, and his stepfather flew to Orlando, Florida, right away.

JOINING A BOY BAND

Timberlake suggested another young singer for the group—nineteen-year-old JC Chasez. Chasez had been a Mouseketeer with Justin on *MMC*. Timberlake thought that Chasez had a good voice and was an excellent dancer. Chasez came to Orlando to audition. He fit right in.

Finally, they found their last two members. One young man was eighteen-year-old Joey Fatone. The last member would be sixteen-year-old Lance Bass.

But the group still didn't have a name. One night the boys, Pearlman, and Justin's mother and stepfather were having dinner at a restaurant. Lynn said, "You know these guys just sound so tight together. They sound very much in synch." Everyone agreed that sounded like a good name. Later, it was shortened to 'N Sync.

▼ *Joey Fatone, Justin Timberlake, Chris Kirkpatrick, Lance Bass, and JC Chasez of 'N Sync pose for a photo in 1998.*

THE BOY BAND CRAZE

Groups such as the Backstreet Boys and 'N Sync are often called "boy bands." So what exactly is a boy band? The term usually refers to a group of young male singers who perform pop music. They often sing in harmony and perform elaborate dance moves.

While many bands come together naturally, a talent manager or record producer often holds auditions to create a boy band. Then they market the group to a preteen and teen audience.

Pearlman had a specific plan to launch the success of 'N Sync. A vocal teacher worked with the boys on their singing and harmonizing. And a choreographer helped them improve their dance skills. Johnny Wright, who managed the Backstreet Boys, was brought in. He set up small concerts for the band at local high schools and at shopping malls. He hoped to build a fan base of school-aged kids.

SUCCESS ON THE WORLD STAGE

Wright then went to Europe to get a record contract for the group. The Backstreet Boys were already a big success there. Wright had no trouble finding a record company interested in 'N Sync. In August 1996, 'N Sync signed a contract with

BMG, a huge German company. In October, the group released its first single record. It was called "I Want You Back." The song became a big hit in Germany.

The band then went on a one-month concert tour as an opening act. In November, they returned to Orlando. It was time to produce the first 'N Sync album. By mid-1997, the group's first album, called *'N Sync*, had been released in Europe. It was a mix of upbeat songs and ballads. The album became a smash hit in Germany and elsewhere in Europe.

The 'N Sync members had become very popular in many foreign countries. But they were still unknown in the United States. Their first album was released in the United States on March 24, 1998. It had some success, but it did not become as popular as the group had hoped. However, the boys were about to get the biggest break of their careers. And they would have the Backstreet Boys to thank for it.

Pop Success

On July 18, 1998, 'N Sync gave a concert at MGM studios in Orlando. The show was the first concert promoted by the Disney Studio. The company had wanted the Backstreet Boys

▲ *Justin Timberlake strikes a pose at the 2002 Grammy Awards.*

to perform. But the band members didn't want to do it. Timberlake and Chasez knew the place very well. They had filmed *The All New Mickey Mouse Club* there. The live 'N Sync concert was recorded and shown on TV several more times. Within a few months, 'N Sync's album had sold a million copies. It stayed in the *Billboard* top ten list for several months.

The rest of the year brought more success. In October, the group toured with Janet Jackson as her opening act. The band also recorded its second album. It was an album of Christmas songs called *Home for Christmas*. In November, 'N Sync began their first U.S. tour as headliners—the main act.

LEGAL PROBLEMS

By the summer of 1999, 'N Sync was the hottest pop music act in the country. The group's first album had sold millions of copies. And its concert dates were bringing in millions of dollars. The boys were making a great deal of money.

The members of 'N Sync had a disagreement with Lou Pearlman. They felt he was taking in more profits than he should have been. This led to a legal dispute. Eventually the

POP SENSATION

Around the turn of the millennium, it seemed as though 'N Sync was everywhere. At the peak of its popularity, 'N Sync performed at the Academy Awards, the World Series, the Super Bowl, and the Olympics. The group recorded or performed songs with Aerosmith, Britney Spears, Michael Jackson, Celine Dion, Stevie Wonder, and Gloria Estefan. The members even appeared as themselves on *The Simpsons*!

two sides came to an agreement. 'N Sync was able to sign with a new record company. Pearlman still received some money, but he was no longer personally involved with the band.

REACHING THE TOP

By the beginning of 2000, 'N Sync seemed to be everywhere on the pop music scene. The boys made the cover of *Rolling Stone* magazine. They appeared on the TV show *Saturday Night Live*. They were nominated for three Grammy Awards and appeared as presenters on the show that year.

Timberlake had become the most well known of the five members. One reason for this was his very public relationship with another pop superstar, Britney Spears. They had been friends from their days together in *MMC*.

In late 1998, Spears was opening for 'N Sync on their tour. And she and Timberlake began dating.

The third 'N Sync album was released in March 2000. It was titled *No Strings Attached*. It sold 2.4 million copies the first week it was available. It held the number one spot on the *Billboard* magazine charts for eight weeks.

On the album, Timberlake really expanded his musical talent. He even wrote one of the songs. He sang solo on two ballads. And he also played a very active role in the final sound mixing of the album.

▼ *'N Sync accepts the award for favorite musical group or band at the 2001 People's Choice Awards.*

▲ *Justin Timberlake answers questions from the media during the Super Bowl halftime show in 2001.*

By the end of 2000, 'N Sync was the world's highest-earning pop music group. They earned more than $267 million in U.S. album sales and on tours.

A NEW DIRECTION

In January 2001, 'N Sync got ready to make a new album. It was titled *Celebrity*. The five members decided to take their music in a new direction. Timberlake was a big influence in

GRADUATION DAY

On May 12, 2000, Justin Timberlake returned to Memphis to perform with 'N Sync. By then the group was very popular. That night 20,000 young music fans jammed into the Pyramid Arena to see the show. Besides the concert, they got to see a surprise event. They saw a high school graduation.

Timberlake had joined 'N Sync when he was fourteen, so he never went to high school. For years he had taken special high school courses and worked with tutors. In September 1999, he received a high school diploma. It was sent to him in the mail. But his mother, Lynn, never gave it to him. Instead, she planned a special graduation ceremony.

Two of his favorite tutors, Chuck Yerger and Brenda Crenshaw, flew in for the event. During a break in the show, Crenshaw walked on stage. Timberlake was shocked. "Justin, we've been trying to catch up with you," Crenshaw told him. "But you've been so busy on the road that we haven't been able to give you your diploma. So we finally came here tonight to do that."

Then Yerger came out. Timberlake ran across the stage and hugged him. Timberlake was given a cap and gown. The other 'N Sync members were given caps too. Then Yerger made a short speech, congratulating Timberlake on his achievement. When he finished, Justin and the band all threw their caps in the air, and the audience cheered. Timberlake couldn't stop smiling.

this decision. Growing up near Memphis, he had heard a lot of rhythm and blues music. Now, he wanted the group to add a real R&B flavor to the new album. The group brought in some experienced R&B producers. Timberlake cowrote seven of the songs.

In May, the group set out on a national tour to promote the new album. The band appeared in large outdoor sports stadiums. They needed fifty trucks and twenty-four buses to carry all the equipment and people from city to city.

The show was spectacular. The group gave one concert at Shea Stadium in New York. A writer for the *Newark Star-Ledger* described what happened during one song. "The five members of 'N Sync flew on wires from the main stage to a ramp in the middle of the stadium floor. They bucked futuristic mechanical bulls and aired a computer-animated video made especially for the tour. Fireworks lit up the sky, geysers of sparks gushed from the stage."

The tour went on for months. It was a huge success. One report said the group made close to $1 million for each performance. The *Celebrity* album was also a big hit. It went on to sell 5 million copies.

GOING THEIR SEPARATE WAYS

After a break in August, the group resumed the *Celebrity* tour. But changes were already under way. The boys announced they were ready to try other things. Lance Bass and Joey Fatone wanted to pursue acting careers. And Timberlake and Chasez hoped to make it as solo performers.

▲ *Justin Timberlake arrives at the Latin Grammy Awards in 2002.*

The group continued to tour into 2002. But Timberlake's mother, who was co-managing his career, was already talking with Jive Records. The final 'N Sync concert took place that year on April 28 in Orlando. A few days later, Timberlake had his record deal as a solo artist. His career was about to reach even greater heights.

Flying Solo

Even before he started his solo career, Timberlake had become one of the most famous male pop stars in the country. In January 2002, he played in the Bob Hope Golf Classic in Palm Springs, California. Timberlake continued to play often and became quite good at the sport.

Timberlake's other favorite sport is basketball. When he was still in 'N Sync, the group sponsored an annual charity basketball game. The first one was held in 1999. It raised $50,000. The next year's event was even more successful. The game raised $550,000 for charities. Timberlake started one of those charities. It is called The Justin Timberlake Foundation. This group raises money for school music programs around the country.

After Timberlake moved to Los Angeles in August 2002, he joined a Hollywood basketball team. There he played with

◄ *Justin Timberlake performs the song "What Goes Around Comes Around" at the 2007 Grammy Awards.*

MUSICAL INFLUENCES

From the time he was a young boy, Justin Timberlake has loved rhythm and blues music, also known as R&B. R&B is a style of music that combines elements of jazz, gospel, and blues music. It dates back to the 1940s. Modern R&B also has influences from soul, funk, and dance music. It features a more electronic sound with heavy drum rhythms and more of a rock feel.

When he was growing up in Tennessee, Timberlake was often surrounded by R&B. As he became a musician, he began putting the R&B sound into his own music.

It was at Timberlake's suggestion that 'N Sync changed its "boy band" sound. On the album *Celebrity*, he co-wrote and helped produce many of the songs. All of these songs showed a strong R&B influence. When he became a solo artist, Timberlake continued that trend. Working with Brian McKnight and Timbaland, Timberlake created records with a modern dance beat combined with the traditional R&B sound.

actors Tobey Maguire, Leonardo DiCaprio, and Jamie Foxx.

A NEW SOUND

Around this time, Timberlake and Britney Spears ended their relationship. Timberlake got over the breakup by focusing on his music. He decided to keep some of the same sound from the last 'N Sync album. He called on R&B singer Brian McKnight to help produce the album. Timberlake also asked hip-hop artist Timbaland and his writing partner Scott Storch to work on the record. Timbaland and Storch wrote the

▲ *Justin Timberlake performs for a sellout crowd in Ireland in 2007.*

music for "Cry Me a River," and Timberlake wrote the song's lyrics. It became the biggest hit on the album.

Timberlake cowrote all thirteen songs on the album. The record had a more mature sound than anything 'N Sync had done. There was even a Latin-flavored dance song called "Señorita."

The album was called *Justified*. It was released on November 5, 2002. Timberlake performed live in Times Square in New York to promote the album. In its first week, the album sold 445,000 copies. Eventually, the record sold 7 million copies.

MUSIC CREDITS

With 'N Sync
'N Sync (1998)
Home for Christmas (1998)
No Strings Attached (2000)
Celebrity (2001)
Greatest Hits (2005)

Solo
Justified (2002)
FutureSex/LoveSounds (2006)

Some critics complained that Timberlake was ripping off other artists or trying to be someone he was not. But Timberlake never made a secret of how much he loved R&B music. His favorite singers growing up were Donny Hathaway, Al Green, Marvin Gaye, Stevie Wonder, and Michael Jackson. Still, the criticism bothered him. He didn't want to be called a copycat.

ON THE ROAD

In May 2003, Timberlake went on the road. He spent almost the entire year on tour. He even teamed up for a while with his old *MMC* costar, Christina Aguilera. Timberlake had a new look. His familiar blond curls were gone. Now he sported a buzz cut. Soon, his fan base was changing as well. His fans were no longer just those who loved him in 'N Sync.

His music was beginning to appeal to people his own age and older. The year ended on a high note. In a December 2003 cover story, *Rolling Stone* called Timberlake "The New King of Pop."

In 2004, Timberlake had the chance to sing for a huge audience. He agreed to perform during the halftime show at the Super Bowl on February 1. He sang a duet with Janet Jackson. In addition to the football fans present, about 90 million people were watching on TV.

A week later, Timberlake returned to the spotlight. On February 8, he won two major Grammy Awards. He won Best Male Pop Vocal Performance for "Cry Me a River." And he won Best Pop Vocal Album for *Justified*.

▶ *Justin Timberlake arrives at the British Music Awards in 2003.*

New Career Paths

In mid-2005, Timberlake took a break from singing. In May, he had surgery. He had some growths removed from his throat. He was told not to strain his voice for several months. During this time, Timberlake hoped to finally launch his acting career. In 2005, he hosted an episode of the popular TV show *Saturday Night Live*. He appeared in a comedy and dancing skit with comedian Jimmy Fallon. Together they spoofed the famous 1970s disco band, the Bee Gees. The skit was a huge hit. Hollywood's movie people took notice.

Later that year, Timberlake got his first role in a major movie. He played a journalist in *Edison Force*, a crime drama. His costars were two major actors: Morgan Freeman and Kevin Spacey. But, the movie never made it to the theaters.

Timberlake had much better success with his next film. It was called *Alpha Dog*. It was based on a true-life crime story.

◀ *Justin Timberlake performs at a Madonna concert in 2008.*

Timberlake played a young man named Frankie Ballenbacher. The film got mixed reviews. But critics raved about Timberlake's performance. TV movie critic Richard Roeper also liked the performance. "Justin Timberlake has what it takes to be a genuine movie star," Roeper wrote. Timberlake was nominated for Breakout Performance in both the MTV and Teen Choice movie awards.

Timberlake continued to work on his movie career over the next several months. He had a supporting role in two dramas. One was called *Black Snake Moan*. It also starred Christina Ricci and Samuel L. Jackson. The other movie was called *Southland Tales*. In both films, Timberlake played soldiers. Justin even got involved in the very popular *Shrek* animated series. He was the voice of the young King Arthur, Artie, in *Shrek the Third*.

A RETURN TO MAKING MUSIC

In December 2005, Timberlake went back into the studio to make another solo album. He asked Timbaland to help him again. The songs they made continued to have an R&B influence. But they also had a harder, more rock 'n' roll feel.

▲ *Justin Timberlake takes a swing while filming the movie* The Open Road.

The album's title was *FutureSex/Love Sounds*. The record was released in September 2006. It opened in the number one position on the *Billboard* charts. It sold 684,000 copies the first week. By early 2007, it had sold more than 6 million copies. Songs on the album ranged from ballads to flashy dance numbers.

Timberlake spent the rest of 2006 and much of 2007 touring. The tour took him across the United States. He also traveled to Canada, Europe, and Australia. He had truly become a world star.

MOVIE CREDITS

Since getting a taste of acting on *The All New Mickey Mouse Club*, Justin Timberlake wanted to try performing in front of the camera again. In 1999, he started getting a few small parts on TV shows. Soon Timberlake had offers to appear in full-length Hollywood films. Below is a list of the films he has appeared in:

Edison Force (2005)
Alpha Dog (2006)
Southland Tales (2006)
Black Snake Moan (2006)
Shrek the Third (2007)
The Love Guru (2008)
The Open Road (2008)

In February 2008, Timberlake again was a Grammy Award winner. He won two awards for *FutureSex/Love Sounds*. He won Best Male Pop Performance for "What Goes Around . . . Comes Around." And he won the Dance Recording Award for "LoveStoned/I Think She Knows."

MANY INTERESTS

Even while making hit music, Timberlake has found time for his many other interests. In 2006, he and childhood friend Trace Ayala started a clothing line. It features such items as sweatshirts, T-shirts, and jeans. Timberlake even played a role in designing some of the clothes.

Timberlake also began his own record company in 2007. Tennman Records was created as a joint company with Interscope Records. Timberlake is the head of the company. The company's goal is to bring new talent to the public.

▼ *Justin Timberlake, an avid golfer, plays in the U.S. Open Golf Challenge event in 2008.*

One of the first artists signed by Tennman Records was singer-songwriter Matt Morris. Morris had helped write songs for Timberlake's second solo album.

In 2008, Timberlake was back in front of movie audiences. He had a supporting role in the comedy *The Love Guru*. Timberlake also had another film release that year. It was *The Open Road*. In this movie he had his first starring role. He played the son of a baseball player. Together with his girlfriend, he takes a road trip with his father.

Later that year, Timberlake hosted the ESPY Awards on ESPN. In October, he hosted and played in his own golf tournament. It was called the Justin Timberlake Shriners Hospital for Children Open. Money from the event went to the Shriners Hospital charity.

The golf event was just one of Timberlake's many charitable efforts. For years he has raised money for music education in public schools. In 2008, for example, Timberlake donated $200,000 to promote music education in Memphis. Half of the money went to the Rock 'n' Soul Museum. The other half went to the Memphis Music Foundation. Timberlake also has given his time and money to many other charities.

HONORS

Justin Timberlake has won numerous awards over the years as a recording artist and performer.

2008
- Won two Grammy Awards: Best Male Pop Vocal Performance, Best Dance Recording
- Won NRJ Music Award (France) for Best International Male Artist

2007
- Won two Grammy Awards: Best Dance Recording (with Timbaland), Best Rap/Sung Collaboration (with T.I.)
- Won two American Music Awards: Favorite Pop/Rock Male Artist, Favorite R&B/Soul Album
- Won British Phonographic Industry Award for Best International Male Artist
- Won Emmy Award for Outstanding Original Music and Lyrics

2004
- Won two Grammy Awards: Best Pop Vocal Album, Best Male Pop Vocal Performance
- Won two British Phonographic Industry Awards: Best International Male Artist, Best International Album

2003
- Won American Music Award for Favorite Pop/Rock Album

STAYING ACTIVE

Justin Timberlake continues to weigh his career choices. He's already found success both as a solo musician and as an actor. It's hard to say what the future holds for this former Mouseketeer. At times, he has talked about quitting the music business. But that doesn't mean he wouldn't do something else.

Timberlake was interviewed by *EW* online magazine in 2007. The interviewer asked him about his plans for the future. "I'm constantly inspired by new things . . . and I don't know that I'll ever retire," Timberlake responded. "I'll just find new things to inspire me."

Justin Timberlake smiles during a press conference in 2006. ▶

Timeline

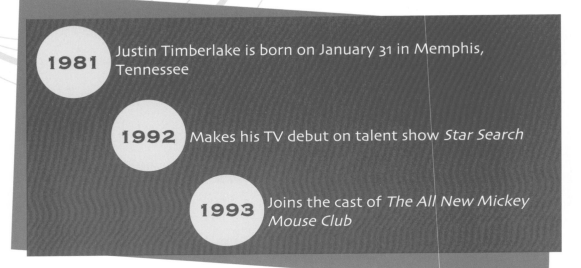

1981 Justin Timberlake is born on January 31 in Memphis, Tennessee

1992 Makes his TV debut on talent show *Star Search*

1993 Joins the cast of *The All New Mickey Mouse Club*

1995 Recruited for a new boy band, which is later named 'N Sync

1998 The first 'N Sync album, *'N Sync*, is released in the United States

2000 The third 'N Sync album, *No Strings Attached*, sells 2.4 million copies in its first week

2002 Releases his first solo album, *Justified*

2003 Called "The New King of Pop" by *Rolling Stone* magazine

2004 Wins two Grammy Awards for *Justified*

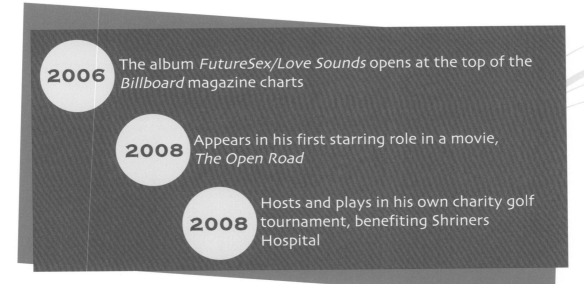

2006 The album *FutureSex/Love Sounds* opens at the top of the *Billboard* magazine charts

2008 Appears in his first starring role in a movie, *The Open Road*

2008 Hosts and plays in his own charity golf tournament, benefiting Shriners Hospital

Further Info

BOOKS

Cefry, Holly. *Justin Timberlake*. New York: Rosen, 2008.

Dougherty, Terri. *Justin Timberlake*. Farmington Hills, MI: Lucent Books, 2008.

Laslo, Cynthia. *'N Sync*. New York: Children's Press, 2000.

Marcovitz, Hal. *Justin Timberlake*. Broomall, PA: Mason Crest, 2007.

CDS AND DVDS

'N Sync: PopOdyssey Live. Jive, 2002.

Shrek the Third. DreamWorks Animated, 2007.

INTERNET ADDRESSES

Justin Timberlake
www.justintimberlake.com

The Justin Timberlake Foundation
www.amc-music.com/partners/timberlake.htmm

Internet Movie Database: Justin Timberlake
www.imdb.com/name/nm0005493

Glossary

audition—A short test of an entertainer's abilities.

celebrity—A famous person.

choreographer—Someone who arranges dance steps or movements for a show.

contract—A legal agreement between people or companies stating the terms by which one will work for the other.

journalist—Someone who collects information and writes articles for newspapers, television, or radio.

lip-synch—To pretend to sing along with a recording.

sketch—A short play that is performed on stage or on television.

solo—A piece of music that is played or sung by one person.

spoof—To make fun of something, often in a humorous skit.

Index